A Sticky Surprise

"That's perfect!" Crystal said. "We'll mix a pile of ants with a glob of peanut butter, then spread it in a sandwich and give it to Frank. That's the perfect peanut butter trap."

"It won't work," Marcie argued. "Frank won't eat an ant sandwich."

Crystal grinned. "I didn't know he put bubble gum in my hair. Maybe Frank won't know about the ants." She giggled. "We'll plan it so he doesn't know until *after* he's eaten them."

"Crystal, that's disgusting," Marcie said. Then she smiled. "Let's do it."

The PEANUT BUTTER TRAP

The
PEANUT BUTTER
TRAP

by Elaine Moore

illustrated by
Meredith Johnson

little rainbow
Troll

Text copyright © 1996 by Elaine Moore.
Cover illustration copyright © 1996 by Troll Communications L.L.C.

Published by Little Rainbow, an imprint and trademark of
Troll Communications L.L.C.

Printed in the United States of America.

10 9 8 7 6 5 4 3

Chapter

1

Frank McCormick was turning himself into a mummy. He was standing next to Crystal and mummifying himself right before her very eyes. It was a good thing her best friends, Angela and Marcie, were working with her at the papier-mâché center so they could witness Frank's latest weird thing.

Frank was supposed to be making a butterfly with Samir. But Samir was doing all the work. His butterfly looked excellent. Crystal had even told him so.

She had pushed her beautiful shiny brown waist-length braids over her shoulder and said, "You are going to get an A plus on that butterfly, Samir. It is so beautiful!"

It was right then that Frank began wrapping his arm in gluey, drippy strips of newspaper.

Angela and Marcie took one look at Frank and started to giggle.

"Don't laugh at him," Crystal insisted. "It only makes him worse. Frank's going to get all of us in T-R-O-U-B-L-E."

Crystal glanced toward the front of the classroom. Ms. Reilly was busy sliding papers in their Going Home folders. The rest of the kids were busy at one of the science centers. The class was doing a unit on Cocoons to Butterflies in science.

"Frank!" Ms. Reilly's voice rang out. "Obviously, you're not ready to work in a team with papier-mâché. Please return to your desk. Perhaps there will be an opening at one of the other centers before the bell rings. You may take a book from the research corner along with you."

Crystal watched as Frank sullenly unwrapped the papier-mâché strips from around his wrist and dropped them in the bucket. He picked up a book and made dinosaur-in-the-swamp stomping noises all the way to his desk.

A few minutes later Crystal walked over to Ms. Reilly.

"I'm finished with my mobile for now. Is it okay if I work on my report cover?"

"Sure," Ms. Reilly answered.

Crystal sat down at her desk. She liked how the classroom buzzed with activity. Except for Frank, who was pushing paper clips into a long line on his desk, everyone was doing something about butterflies or caterpillars.

Crystal reached inside her desk for her 102 shades of Hearts-A-Glo markers. She set them up like an easel. What colors should she use for the butterfly's wing tips? Which would make a better thorax? New Spring Green or Pale Raspberry Sorbet?

Plip!

A paper clip landed in the bright patch of sunlight on the floor beside Crystal's sneaker.

Frank McCormick was at it again.

Crystal squared her shoulders and reached for Pale Raspberry Sorbet. It was the perfect color for the fourteen hearts she had drawn on the edge of each wing. Humming quietly to herself, Crystal pushed her braids out of the way and set to work.

Plip!

Crystal's hand jerked. Oh, no! Instead of fourteen hearts, she had thirteen hearts and a blob. Crystal scowled.

"Frank! Quit it!" She whirled around just as Frank flicked another paper clip. The paper clips were supposed to be for the papier-mâché mobiles. Leave it to Frank to use them as ammunition aimed right at her.

Plip!

"Stop it, Frank!"

Frank rubbed his hand through the cowlick over his right eyebrow. He gave Crystal a lopsided grin. Then he held up both hands.

"All gone!"

Sometimes Frank sounded like Angela's little brother. But Angela's little brother was three and cute. Frank wasn't three. And he definitely wasn't cute!

Crystal went back to her drawing.

Pop! Chomp, chomp, chomp. *Pop!*

Crystal turned around and glared at Frank. What weird thing was he doing now?

He was sitting scrunched in his chair with his knees drawn up almost to his shoulders, jerking his head and making crunching noises. Any minute Crystal expected him to fall off his chair and wiggle around on the floor.

"What are you doing?"

"I'm a caterpillar chomping my way out of my cocoon. Couldn't you tell?" He pretended to eat dribbles of papier-mâché off his fingers.

Chomp, chomp, chomp. *Pop!*

"No, I couldn't tell. Anyway, caterpillars don't chew grape bubble gum." Crystal hoped the bubble would explode on Frank's face and make his nose yucky. It would serve him right.

Chomp, chomp, chomp. *Pop!*

Crystal couldn't stand it any longer. She turned in her chair and faced him. "Frank! Park it!"

"Park what?"

"Your bubble gum. You're chomping in my ear."

"You want me to swallow it? You want me to choke?"

Frank put his hands around his neck like he was choking. His head fell against his shoulder. His tongue flopped out, limp and gross, while his head shook from side to side.

"Frank McCormick, you are a disgusting eepy-creepy nightmare!"

Frank stopped choking. From the lopsided grin on his face, Crystal guessed her insult was exactly what he wanted to hear.

What a pain!

Crystal turned around and flipped back her long brown braids just as Ms. Reilly stood up.

"Frank, if you want to join me at the observation center, I'm ready to give you a second chance. I need someone to help me tally up the number of butterflies that have hatched today before we cover them up for the night."

Crystal smiled smugly to herself. Now Ms. Reilly would see that Frank was chewing gum. And chewing gum was not allowed in the classroom.

Now Frank was really going to get in T-R-O-U-B-L-E.

Frank's chair squeaked as he got up. On his way to the observation center, he gave one of Crystal's braids a hard yank.

Crystal didn't scream. She didn't stick out her tongue either. Maybe if she ignored Frank, he would stop being such a pest.

A few minutes later, Angela sat down in the desk next to Crystal. She had finished her papier-mâché butterfly. Crystal rolled her eyes and nodded in Frank's direction.

"Mr. Weird is being a real jerk," she mumbled.

"Yeah, weirder and jerkier than usual."

"Class, we have ten minutes to clean up," Ms. Reilly called out. "It's almost time for dismissal, and I need to hand out your folders."

A few minutes later Crystal threw her backpack across her desk and shoved her Going Home folder inside.

"Walkers, you're dismissed," Ms. Reilly called out. "Have a pleasant afternoon."

Crystal picked up her backpack and started out the door along with Marcie and Angela.

Ever since first grade, Crystal, Marcie, and Angela had walked home from school together. They all lived on top of a hill right off Brandywine Avenue in Rosetree Court. After school the girls usually played together and visited each other's houses. If one of them had to go someplace, the other two girls usually went along. They were like the Three Musketeers — all for one and one for all.

The buses were already in a line at the curb. The Three Musketeers turned left and headed toward the corner where a crossing guard would help them cross Brandywine Avenue.

Lots of other kids lived near their school. There were lots of kids walking or riding their bikes through the neighborhood.

Crystal, Marcie, and Angela were on Brandywine Avenue when Crystal slipped her arm through the loop on her backpack. She flipped one braid over her shoulder to get it out of the way. When she started to flip the other braid, her hand touched something sticky.

"Oh, yuck!" Crystal shouted. "That awful Frank McCormick must have stuck papier-mâché in my hair! Rats! I just shampooed it yesterday. Now I've got to do it all over again. Frank McCormick is the biggest pain!"

"Let me see," Marcie demanded.

"Oh my gosh, Crystal." Marcie stepped back in shock. "Look, Angela. Do you want to tell her?"

Angela placed both her hands on her heart. Her brown eyes got as big as saucers. "Not me. I could never. . ."

"Tell me what?" Crystal shrieked. "What?"

Marcie put her hands on her hips. She clucked her tongue. "It's not papier-mâché, Crystal. It's bubble gum. It's halfway up and it's stuck clear through your braid."

Oh, no! A sinking feeling settled in Crystal's stomach. That stupid Frank McCormick had parked his bubble gum all right. He'd parked it in her hair!

How would her mother ever get the bubble gum out of her hair? What if she had to cut it? Crystal's hair had never been cut, not since she was a baby.

What if Crystal had to have all her hair cut off— all because of that stupid Frank McCormick?

Chapter

2

"**W**hat are you going to do, Crystal?" Marcie exclaimed. "It's not even ordinary pink bubble gum. It's grape! And grape bubble gum is the worst. It's like Super-Glue."

"Let me look again." Angela pushed against Marcie to examine Crystal's braids. "Ooh, Crystal," she moaned. "It even has gross teeth marks in it."

Marcie peeked underneath Crystal's braid. "This is the pits," she said. "Do you know how I know grape is like Super-Glue?"

Crystal was too afraid to ask. She tried to imagine how she'd look with her hair cut as short as Marcie's. Probably awful.

Marcie went on. "You know our cocker spaniel, Inky?"

Crystal and Angela nodded.

"When he got grape bubble gum in his fur, my mom had to take him to the groomers. They had to shave Inky down to the *skin*."

Angela screamed.

Crystal gulped. She reached around to touch the back of her head right where the barber's clippers would start buzzing her hair. Her heart sank down to her knees.

The next time Frank called her Crystal Ball, it wouldn't be because of her name. It would be because her head was smooth and shiny.

Angela put her arm around Crystal's shoulders. "Don't worry. Your mom is cool. She'll think of something."

Crystal shut her eyes and tried not to cry. She better not see Frank McCormick anytime soon.

Just then Marcie shouted, "Well, would you look who's coming."

Crystal opened her eyes as Frank and his friends Davy and Shawn zoomed toward them on their bikes. Frank led the way. He had his red jacket tied around his neck, and it flapped behind him in the breeze.

"He probably thinks he's Superman," Crystal said under her breath.

"Except Superman is nice," said Angela.

"Anyone who would put horrible grape bubble gum in someone's hair is just plain nasty," Marcie announced.

Frank waited until he saw the girls watching. Then he did a wheelie. And when he got closer to where they were standing, he leaned back, held his head high, and folded his arms across his chest. What a show-off!

Marcie took a step closer to the curb. She put her hands on her hips and yelled, "I hope you crash, Frank!"

"Yeah," shouted Angela. "For what you did to Crystal."

"Shhh!" Crystal cringed. She didn't want the whole world to know that Frank McCormick had managed to smush grape bubble gum in her hair.

"We're not even going to talk to you dumb boys," Marcie yelled when Shawn and Davy parked their bikes at the curb.

"Yeah," Angela yelled even louder. "You might give us germs, and we don't want any."

The Three Musketeers hurried up the hill, leaving the two boys behind.

But Frank pumped the pedals of his bike as hard as he could. He cruised up into a driveway, made a sharp turn, and sailed down the sidewalk. Then he came to a screeching stop about six inches in front of Crystal's big toe.

"Knock it off, Frank!" Crystal scowled at him.

Frank was out of breath from pumping so hard. He sat on his bike, panting like a puppy, and grinned at Crystal.

"That was a gross, disgusting thing you did with your bubble gum, Frank," Marcie said.

Frank didn't pay any attention to Marcie. Instead he looked straight at Crystal and grinned even wider.

"Did you get my present?" he asked innocently.

"Present?" Crystal frowned. "What present? You call a handful of chewed-up bubble gum a present?"

Frank brushed the cowlick over his eye. "Oh, that? That wasn't the present. I just parked it, like you told me to." His dimple flashed. "The present is in your backpack."

"What kind of present?" Marcie butted in.

Crystal slipped her backpack off her shoulders and set it on the sidewalk.

Frank squeezed the brakes on his handlebars. "I think you'll like it. It's really neat."

Crystal eyeballed Frank. A little voice told her to be careful.

She pulled back the flap, opened it up, and reached inside. She moved her hand around.

"Frank, there's nothing . . ."

Suddenly her fingers touched something cold and damp.

"Eeeeeaaaaahh!" Crystal screamed, yanking her hand free. She jumped back. Something was moving inside her backpack!

"It's alive!" Marcie yelled, grabbing Angela's elbow.

Just then a green frog hopped out of the backpack onto the grass.

Shawn and Davy rode up on their bikes and doubled over with laughter. They stomped around on the sidewalk and slapped their knees, as if scaring girls was the funniest thing in the world.

Marcie was madder than ever. "For your information, Cocoon Head, that is a dumb present," she hollered at Frank. "It's bad enough that Crystal's got a mess of gross gum in her hair. Now she's going to get warts. You are the absolute worst, Frank McCormick!"

"Yeah," Angela piped up. "She'll have so many warts she won't be able to do her homework."

Frank didn't care. He and the other boys were too busy making stupid frog noises.

"Come on, you guys. I have to get home." Crystal wiped her hands on her shirt. Then she grabbed her backpack and hurried up the hill toward Rosetree Court.

Any other afternoon she might have noticed the pretty gardens and flowering shrubs. Not today. Now all Crystal could think of was bees. If she didn't walk fast enough, the bees would smell the horrible grape bubble gum in her hair and sting her. And it was all thanks to that stupid, weird, bratty Frank McCormick!

Crystal put her head down and walked as fast as she could. She took a shuddering breath and tried hard not to cry. She hadn't been bald since she was a little baby.

"Mom!" Crystal wailed at the top of her lungs the minute she burst inside the front door. "Look what Frank McCormick did."

She held her braid straight out so her mother could see.

"It's grape," Marcie volunteered. "That's the worst kind. If you don't believe me, you can ask my mom."

Mrs. Gibbons raised her eyebrows. "Thank you, Marcie," she said. "But this time I think I'd rather call Frank's mother."

Crystal took a step back. "But Mom!" she pleaded.

"Well, someone has to speak to Frank," Mrs. Gibbons said. "The next time I see him, I'll speak to him myself."

Crystal blinked. "But you can fix my hair, can't you, Mom?"

Mrs. Gibbons turned Crystal's braid over in her hand and examined the wad of bubble gum.

"Well, at least he didn't get the bubble gum any closer

19

to your hairline," she said as she turned the matted section over in her hand. "And it's only in one braid and not in both. I suppose we should be thankful for that. This is bad enough."

Crystal pulled her good braid over her shoulder and stroked it lovingly. She wondered how she would look with short hair on one half of her head and a long braid on the other half. Probably lopsided!

Maybe she could do what Marcie's father did to cover up his bald spot. She could comb her long hairs over to the other side of her head. Maybe she could twirl her only remaining braid around her head like a turban.

Crystal squeezed her eyes tight to keep from crying. No matter what she did, thanks to Frank McCormick, she was going to look really stupid.

"Come on, girls." Mrs. Gibbons lifted Crystal's backpack off the floor. "Fortunately, I grew up in a family with lots of brothers and sisters. So I know all about bubble gum," she said as she gently led Crystal toward the kitchen.

"That's good," Angela murmured.

"But that was a long time ago. They probably didn't have *grape* back then. I keep telling you, grape is *definitely* the worst," Marcie said.

Crystal's heart plunged clear down to her toes. Her mom could fix almost anything. Could she fix Frank McCormick's latest mess?

Mrs. Gibbons squeezed Crystal's shoulder. She turned toward Marcie and Angela. "Are you girls staying for the operation? Then you had better call home first.

Your mothers have to know where you are."

Mrs. Gibbons motioned for Crystal to climb on top of a stool. She gave a large fluffy towel a good shake and draped it across Crystal's shoulders.

"Let's see. First we'll need this," Mrs. Gibbons announced. She set a big jar of creamy peanut butter on the counter. "And, we have to have a shiny spoon. Get that for me, please, Angela. And in a moment we'll need an ice cube. Marcie, be ready!"

Marcie cleared her throat and stepped forward. "Excuse me, Mrs. Gibbons, but we can wait for our snack until after you operate on Crystal."

Mrs. Gibbons smiled at Marcie. She sunk the spoon deep in the jar of peanut butter. "Oh, I'm not fixing a snack."

And with that she slathered great gooey gobs of peanut butter all over Crystal's braid.

"Oooooooh!" Angela exclaimed.

"Mom! What are you doing?" Crystal yelled. She felt her mom's fingers gently knead the peanut butter through her hair.

"Marcie!" Mrs. Gibbons reached back with her open hand. "Ice, please."

The peanut butter made squishy noises next to Crystal's ear. Cool drops of water dribbled down her neck. Angela and Marcie couldn't stop staring. Slowly Mrs. Gibbons coaxed tiny bits of gum out of Crystal's long hair.

"I didn't know peanut butter was good for that," Marcie said.

"My sister puts my father's beer in her hair," Angela piped up. "She's sixteen and she says beer makes her hair shiny. And my father puts peanut butter in mousetraps."

"You have mice in your house?" Crystal asked.

"Not anymore." Angela covered her mouth with her hands. "Oops! I think it was supposed to be a secret."

Crystal's mother laughed. "Don't worry, sweetie. Your secret is safe with us."

"Frank McCormick practically lives on peanut butter," Marcie said. "I spend all day smelling his peanut butter breath."

"It sounds like he must love the stuff," Mrs. Gibbons said.

"He adores it," Marcie said. "Instead of buying lunch in the cafeteria, he always brings a peanut butter sandwich in a brown paper bag. His grandmother makes them. Every day it's peanut butter, peanut butter, peanut butter. He never gets tired of it."

"Who cares what Frank likes," said Crystal. "He hates me."

"Oh, no, darling." Mrs. Gibbons wiped her hands on the towel and wrapped her arms around Crystal. "Frank probably likes you. You have a brother. You know how silly boys can act."

Crystal sniffed. "I do know, but I still say Frank doesn't like me. And I certainly don't like Frank."

Mom gazed into Crystal's eyes for a long time before loosening the other braid.

"Sometimes, especially in third grade, boys don't

know how to say or show that they like a girl. They do silly things, but they don't think they're being mean." Mrs. Gibbons paused. "Unless someone's mother tells them, which I intend to do."

Marcie pursed her lips and squinted. "Well, if Frank liked Crystal, he would have said he was sorry."

"Maybe," Mrs. Gibbons said.

"Yuck," Marcie said crossly.

"Yuck," repeated Angela.

"Yuck, yuck, and double yuck!" Crystal made a face like a bowl full of spinach. She didn't want anyone as weird as Frank McCormick to like her. That would make her weird too.

"Come on, girls." Mrs. Gibbons helped Crystal off the stool. "We'll finish up in the laundry room."

Crystal bent her head over the laundry tub and watched the soapy bubbles swirl around her hair before disappearing down the drain.

Boy, was she lucky! Her mother was probably the only one in the world who knew how to get grape bubble gum out of someone's hair without shaving the person bald. What if her mother hadn't known about using peanut butter? Instead of bubbles, it would have been her hair sliding down the drain!

Crystal's cheeks turned warm. If Frank actually did like her, he had a strange way of showing it.

While Mrs. Gibbons braided Crystal's hair, Angela and Marcie fixed a tray of peanut butter and crackers.

"Thanks, Mom," Crystal whispered. "You're the best."

The girls carried their snack outside to their usual

spot, under a towering oak tree in Crystal's backyard.

"If you ask me," Angela said, "Frank should say he's sorry twice—once for the bubble gum, twice for the frog."

Crystal nodded. "He never says he's sorry, though. Not when he put the snowball down my jacket. Not when he made a paper airplane out of my book report. Not even when he sailed my book report out the classroom window."

Marcie chewed on a cracker. She looked very thoughtful. "If Frank won't say he's sorry, we shouldn't wait for your mother to take care of him. We should do something right away to *make* him sorry."

"Like what?"

Crystal scraped the peanut butter off her cracker with her finger and licked it clean. She didn't like to fight with people. She was probably the only kid who didn't fight with her brother. But maybe Marcie was right. Maybe Frank did need to learn a lesson.

"Hey, you guys," Crystal said slowly while carefully examining her finger. "If Angela's dad can trap mice with peanut butter, the Three Musketeers ought to be able to trap a rat like Frank." She raised her eyebrows in a knowing way. "We could *make* him say he's sorry."

"Yeah, but how?"

"Well," Crystal said. "Frank likes peanut butter, right? So we could make him a really yucky sandwich."

Marcie's eyes practically popped out of her head. "Peanut butter and mice between bread?" she asked.

Crystal paused to brush an ant off her leg. "No, mice

wouldn't work. But we can still trap Frank with peanut butter and something really gross."

Marcie frowned like she wasn't sure. She helped herself to more crackers. "What's gross about peanut butter? Peanut butter is like chocolate. You can't do anything bad with chocolate."

"Yes, you can," Angela said. "I saw a can of chocolate-covered ants in the deli. That's gross."

"Wow!" Crystal exploded. "That's perfect! We'll mix a pile of ants with a glob of peanut butter, then spread it in a sandwich and give it to Frank. That's the perfect peanut butter trap."

Marcie let out a long breath. "It won't work," she argued. "You're forgetting something. Frank won't eat an ant sandwich."

Crystal grinned. "I didn't know he put bubble gum in my hair. Maybe Frank won't know about the ants." She giggled. "We'll plan it so he doesn't know until *after* he's eaten them."

"Crystal, that's disgusting," Marcie said. Then she smiled. "Let's do it."

Chapter

3

Crystal folded her arms across her chest and scowled. "There's not one anthill in this whole backyard. Where are ants when you really need them?"

Setting a peanut butter trap for mice might be a snap. But making a peanut butter trap for Frank was hard!

"I haven't seen any ants except for the one that was crawling up my leg when we were eating crackers." Crystal pouted.

"Don't forget the ones we found wandering around on your back porch," Angela reminded her.

She tapped the plastic storage bowl Crystal had given her. Inside were two miserable ants. She opened the lid slightly so the ants could get some air.

When she did, Marcie stomped her foot. "Big deal. You can't make an ant sandwich with only two ants. What kind of trap is that? It's too bad we're not on a picnic."

"Hey, what a great idea! Wait here, you guys," Crystal said. "I'll be right back."

Crystal raced up the porch steps and into the kitchen. She opened the refrigerator and reached inside. Perfect!

A few minutes later the Three Musketeers were taking turns dribbling a can of orange soda on the sidewalk.

"Here they come!" Marcie exclaimed.

Hordes of black ants swarmed out of the grass and onto the sidewalk. Quickly the girls scraped them up. They dumped the ants into the plastic bowl.

"Lucky for us your mom had to pick up your big brother from baseball practice," Marcie said as they entered Crystal's house. "Otherwise we'd have a lot of explaining to do."

"If I got caught doing this at my house, my mom would totally lose it," Angela said.

Crystal nodded. "Don't worry. We're not going to get caught."

She pulled a clean spoon out of the drawer and scooped out two spoonfuls of peanut butter. Using her finger, she pushed the peanut butter into the bowl of ants.

Marcie shoved closer. "Don't you do it all," she said when Crystal set the spoon down. "It's my turn."

Angela covered her eyes. "Ooooooh, gross." She stepped away from the counter. "I can't look. Tell me when you're finished."

Crystal watched as Marcie stirred. It didn't take long. Soon little black specks dotted the brown peanut butter.

"Get the bread," Marcie told Angela.

Angela uncovered her eyes. She grabbed the bread out of the refrigerator and set it on the counter. Then she

peeked in the bowl and groaned. "I'm going to be sick. I am really going to be sick." She covered her eyes again.

Crystal took a deep breath. She stuck the spoon into the bowl of peanut butter and ants.

"Spread it on both pieces of bread," Marcie directed. "It's no good unless Frank gets a lot of ants."

"Yeah, like a whole ant colony."

"Ooooooh, gross."

"You have to cut it in half, otherwise Frank will know something's up," Marcie said. "Frank's grandmother always cuts his sandwiches in half."

"She cuts them slanted like a sailboat."

"Yeah. Then Frank sails them into his big mouth."

Crystal picked up a knife. "Okay, here goes. I'm ready to slice it in half."

"Try not to cut through any ants," Angela warned.

"You're not going to be able to tell, silly," said Marcie. "The ants are already smothered." She turned to Crystal. "Do you have a plastic bag? Frank always brings his sandwich to school in a plastic bag."

Crystal pulled a box of plastic bags out of a drawer and handed one to Marcie. "Here, this ought to do it."

Next they put the sandwich in a brown paper lunch bag and stuck it in the refrigerator. All Crystal had to do tomorrow was take the bag to school in her backpack. They'd switch bags in the cafeteria.

Poor Frank. He wouldn't even know what he was eating.

Crystal was thinking hard as she rinsed out the bowl and dried her hands on a towel.

"It would be better if Frank would apologize," she told her friends. "Then we wouldn't have to do this yucky trick."

"You've got to be kidding," Marcie shouted. "A peanut butter and ant sandwich isn't as yucky as putting gross bubble gum in your hair."

"That could have been disastrous!" Angela agreed. "What if your mother had to take you to the dog groomers? What if they shaved your head bald?"

Crystal thought about that. "Maybe we could make Frank say he was sorry so he wouldn't have to eat the ants."

Marcie shook her head. "I doubt you can make him say it."

Angela squeezed her eyes tight, as if she was thinking really hard.

"I know," she said finally. "What if Frank thought Crystal's mother really had to shave her head? What if he thought Crystal really *was* bald? Would he say he was sorry then?"

"If he thought I had warty hands, then he'd be double sorry."

Angela batted her eyelashes. "Especially if he likes you, Crystal. Then he'd be super sorry."

"I think I know how we can make Frank think you're bald," Marcie said. "We can take care of your hands, too. Then if Frank doesn't *say* he's sorry, we'll make him *really, really* sorry."

With that all three girls smiled and gave the thumbs-up sign.

Chapter

4

The next morning, the Three Musketeers met behind a big bush on the corner of Rosetree Court and Brandywine Avenue. Crystal was wearing the new short set she got for her birthday. Angela and Marcie were wearing shorts too. It was going to be a very hot day.

"Do you have Frank's sandwich?" Angela asked.

Crystal tapped her backpack. "In here." She turned toward Marcie. "Give me the hat."

Marcie shoved a heavy knit hat at Crystal. "Here, put it on before anyone sees. Tuck your hair up underneath."

Angela bounced on her feet. "Oh, neat. You really do look bald. Frank is going to feel so sorry for you."

"Here," said Marcie. "Put these mittens on to cover up your make-believe warts."

Crystal tried to scratch under the hat. With mittens on, that was hard to do.

"This better work, you guys," she said. "I'm already beginning to itch. I'm getting sweaty, too."

"It'll work," Marcie promised. "And just to make sure that Birdbrain Frank gets the picture, I wrote him a note." She pulled a spiral binder out of her notebook and opened it to the right page.

Crystal looked over Marcie's shoulder while Angela read the letter out loud.

Dear Frank,
It's all your falt that Crystal is bald and has warts on her hands. You should say your sorry for being such a pea-brain.
Love,
Marcie

Crystal made a face. "You spelled some of the words wrong."

"Big deal. There's no grade. Frank won't even notice."

"I'll bet he notices the word *love*," Angela said in a singsong voice.

Crystal rolled her eyes. "C'mon, you guys. We better hurry if we want to get to school before the bell rings. We don't want to get into T-R-O-U-B-L-E."

But when the girls entered the classroom, Frank was nowhere to be seen.

Crystal backed out the door and into the hall. "Let's hang up our things," she murmured. "Maybe he's in the coat closet."

Frank wasn't.

"Doesn't surprise me," Angela said under her breath. "Frank's always late."

"Okay," Marcie ordered as they returned to the classroom. "This is it. Act normal."

Crystal stared at Marcie. Normal? What was normal about wearing an itchy hat and mittens when you had shorts on?

"No matter what happens, don't take your hat off," Marcie whispered. "Or your mittens, either. That would ruin everything."

Crystal made a beeline past Ms. Reilly and a bunch of other kids. Out of the corner of her eye, she saw some of the kids do a double take. She heard them whispering, too.

She felt awfully weird when she sat down at her desk.

"Class, we have some extra time this morning to continue working on our science projects," Ms. Reilly announced.

Good. Crystal pulled her Hearts-A-Glo markers out of her desk. She needed to finish the cover for her butterfly report.

The problem was, she couldn't get a good grip on the marker. The first time she tried to press the Pale Raspberry Sorbet Hearts-A-Glo marker to the page, it flew out of her hand like a rocket. You probably weren't supposed to work with Hearts-A-Glo markers while wearing woolen mittens.

Angela picked the marker up off the floor and handed it to Crystal. "Remember what Marcie said," she whispered. "No matter what happens, don't take your hat off. Or the mittens, either."

Crystal sighed. That was easy for them to say.

Frank had just plopped down in his chair when Ms. Reilly called, "Crystal, do we have a problem this morning we need to talk about?" She motioned Crystal to the front of the room.

"Oh, you mean my mittens?" Crystal asked politely.

Crystal could feel Frank watching. She knew he was leaning forward, trying to listen. She hoped Marcie remembered to give Frank the note so he would know what was going on.

"Yes, the mittens," Ms. Reilly answered. "And the hat."

The rule about not wearing hats in the classroom flashed through Crystal's head. The principal probably had a rule about mittens, too. Crystal didn't want to get into trouble for breaking a school rule. She needed to think of something quick.

"Um . . ." Crystal stammered. "It's . . . um . . . it's just that I have a dangerously contagious case of poison ivy."

She thought she saw a flicker of a smile on Ms. Reilly's face.

"Of course. But what about your head?" Ms. Reilly prodded. "I certainly hope there's a good reason for the hat, also."

Crystal stepped around to the side of the teacher's desk. She wanted to be sure that Frank could see and hear everything.

"You want to know about my head?" Crystal made her chin quiver. She tried to think of the saddest part of the saddest movie she'd ever seen. Then she gave Ms. Reilly her most woeful look and faked a little sob.

"I'm trying really hard to be brave," she whispered

hoarsely. "But I think I must be having a b-b-bad no-hair day. Please don't make me take the hat off."

Ms. Reilly's eyes widened when Crystal said *no-hair*.

"Oh, Crystal, I'm so sorry. I had no idea," Ms. Reilly apologized. "Go on back to your desk. We'll have to make the best of this, won't we?"

Crystal sniffled. She stared down at her shoes. Then she looked up at Ms. Reilly without moving her head.

"I'll try," she whispered.

Crystal walked slowly back to her desk. She felt lousy for lying.

Crystal sat down and glanced over her shoulder at Frank. He was reading Marcie's note. If she saw the tiniest hint that he was sorry for making her bald, she'd cancel their plan for the peanut butter trap. But when Frank looked up, he didn't even blink. His face just turned red.

But not nearly as red as Crystal's face!

Under the hat, Crystal was hotter than a firecracker on the Fourth of July. Her whole head itched and she could feel beads of sweat dribbling down her flaming-red cheeks. But the mittens were the worst. She'd already messed up the border on her report cover. She had to change the heart border to beach balls, and none of them were the same size. Thanks to Frank, her report cover looked stupid.

When she got a terrible grade for her butterfly report, it would be another bad thing that was all Frank's fault.

It seemed like forever before they got to morning recess.

Out on the playground the Three Musketeers huddled together by the hopscotch game. Crystal wished it was lunchtime so she could give Frank his sandwich.

Suddenly someone snatched the hat off Crystal's head.

"Hey, you!" Frank bellowed. He charged across the playground.

Crystal turned in time to see a big fourth-grade boy running and waving the hat in the air.

Smack! Frank tackled the boy and threw him to the ground.

The two boys were rolling and kicking in the dust when a shrill whistle blew. But Frank didn't stop. He kept grabbing at the hat.

The whistle blew again.

"That will be enough, you two!" A playground aide pulled Frank to his feet. "Give me that hat."

She took the hat from Frank. "Imagine a fight over a woolen hat on a hot day like today. We don't tolerate fighting on the playground for any reason whatsoever. We'll wait for your teachers in the principal's office. I'm recommending detention for both of you."

The aide had a firm grip on Frank's arm. But Frank managed to jerk around as she escorted him and the other boy off the playground.

That was when he saw Crystal standing next to Angela and Marcie. When he noticed her shiny brown braids hanging over her shoulders, his mouth dropped open in shock.

Crystal couldn't think of a thing to say. She could hardly even swallow. She just stood there on the blacktop, fiddling with one of her braids and biting her lower lip.

Marcie put her hand on Crystal's shoulder. "Don't let Frankenstein make you feel bad."

"Yeah," said Angela. "We gave Frank a chance to say he was sorry."

Her friends were probably right. The whole thing was Frank's fault. If anyone deserved the peanut butter trap, Frank sure did.

Chapter

5

Crystal stared at the black hands on the classroom clock. If only they would move faster. She wanted it to be lunchtime so she could give Frank McCormick his very own ant sandwich.

Ever since they'd returned from recess, Frank had been sitting very quietly at his desk. He hadn't thrown one paper clip or spitball. When a pretty yellow-and-brown butterfly escaped from the cage, Frank didn't even grab at it. He looked so sad.

During math Ms. Reilly put problems on the board. Then she walked around the classroom to be sure everyone was getting the answers right. She stopped and tapped Crystal gently on the arm.

"I see your bad no-hair day has gotten better," she said, smiling kindly.

After that, Frank hadn't looked at Crystal, not once. She knew because she'd checked. Every time she'd peeked, Frank was either writing or fumbling around in his desk. He was probably mad because she had tricked him when she hid her braids under the knit hat.

But if Frank had really looked, he would have seen the bulges under the hat. He would have known the bulges were braids. Was it her fault Frank fell for the joke?

Crystal sighed. Too bad for Frank.

Finally Ms. Reilly called the third grade to line up to go to the cafeteria for lunch.

Frank bolted from his chair. He pushed Shawn out of the way and got behind Crystal. Before she could stop him, Frank placed the tip of one of her braids across his upper lip. Then he karate-chopped the air, swinging his arm like a samurai warrior.

Everyone laughed. Except Crystal. Instead of laughing, Crystal tightened her grip on the sandwich bag she'd brought from home. Inside was the ant sandwich. That sandwich was just perfect for weird Frank McCormick.

The Three Musketeers stayed together through the cafeteria line, just like they did every day. But then they did something different. Instead of picking their table first, they waited until the boys sat down. Then they took the table closest to the boys.

Marcie reached inside her lunch bag. "Tell me when they're looking this way."

Crystal whispered the signal. "Now!"

Angela ducked as Marcie tossed a handful of Goldfish crackers under the table. "One, two, three. Sharks!" she screamed at the top of her lungs.

Angela and Crystal jumped back so fast that a chair hit the floor with a loud *bang!*

Shawn and Davy dove under the table. Frank wasn't far behind.

That's when Crystal switched the two lunch bags.

"Dumb girls," the boys muttered as they climbed back into their chairs.

"That's what you think," Marcie said. She raised her eyebrows knowingly at Crystal. Crystal glanced away quickly. She didn't want the boys to suspect anything.

All they had to do now was wait.

Crystal opened her milk carton. She slipped the paper off the straw and pretended to sip her milk while keeping her eyes glued to Frank.

Leave it to Frank to take his time.

First Frank pulled the sandwich out of the bag. Then he blew up the brown paper lunch bag until it popped. He socked Shawn on the arm and shoved Davy with his elbow. His friends shoved him back.

Next Frank ripped open the plastic bag. He pulled out half of the sandwich and started talking to Shawn. Then he took a bite.

The girls tried not to giggle.

Frank went on talking to Shawn.

Crystal couldn't stand it. Frank had the sandwich in his hand. A big bite was missing from it.

Frank turned to say something to Davy.

Crystal shook her head in disbelief.

"What's the matter with him?" she whispered to Angela. "You'd think Frank would do something like throw up or spit out one of the ants."

"Maybe we should have used something bigger, like

grasshoppers," Angela whispered back.

Finally Crystal couldn't stand the suspense any longer. She rapped on the table to get Frank's attention.

"How's your sandwich today?" she asked sweetly.

Frank tilted his head. For a minute he seemed surprised that Crystal was even speaking to him. But he recovered quickly.

"S'okay," he said. "Pretty good, in fact." He took another bite. "Kind of sugary."

From the expression on his face, Crystal could tell Frank was reaching back with his tongue, searching for the peanut butter that was stuck on the roof of his mouth.

"Maybe my grandmother switched brands and forgot to tell me," Frank said slowly. He sounded puzzled. "Usually she doesn't do that. Usually she tells me first. I wonder why she. . ."

Crystal bit down on her lip to keep from laughing out loud. Marcie and Angela were rocking back and forth, hanging on to their chairs.

"It feels like it's got little bits of things in it, sort of . . ."

Finally, thoroughly stumped by the strange new flavor, Frank opened what remained of his sandwich.

He frowned. He bent closer to get a better look.

Crystal had to hold herself tight to keep from laughing. She snuck a quick peek at Marcie and Angela. They were doubled over. Their shoulders started to shake.

"What the. . ." Frank poked a black speck with his finger. He picked it up between his finger and his thumb and laid it across the back of his hand.

For the second time that day, his jaw dropped. He looked at Shawn and Davy.

"Ants?"

"Quick! Spit it out," Shawn yelled. He grabbed a napkin and shoved it at Frank. He started slapping Frank on the back.

Davy grabbed the other half of Frank's sandwich. He peeled the bread apart.

"Who did this to you?" Davy asked Frank. "What did you do to deserve this?"

The girls couldn't stand it any longer. They exploded into gales of laughter.

Frank stopped choking. He pushed Shawn away.

"Y-you?" he stammered. "Crystal?"

Chapter

6

Slowly Frank pushed his chair back from the table and stood up. Crystal's heart pounded in her chest. For a long minute, she thought Frank might strangle her with her braids.

Instead, Frank bowed low and deep, as if he was Prince Charming and Crystal was Snow White. "Why thank you, Crystal," he said in a loud, clear voice. "Thank you for making me such a delicious sandwich. I didn't know you cared."

Crystal's mouth dropped. What was he talking about? She never said she cared for Frank McCormick!

Frank wasn't finished. "Are you going to make me another sandwich tomorrow?" he said.

Marcie puffed herself up. "We haven't decided yet, insect breath."

"I'd *love* peanut butter and banana," Frank went on, ignoring Marcie.

"What about peanut butter and tomato?" Shawn interrupted.

Davy leaned across the table and grinned. "Or peanut butter and marshmallow, or mayonnaise, or . . ."

Frank stared at the ceiling, rubbing his chin thoughtfully. "I tell you what." He pointed his finger right at Crystal. "Why don't you surprise me."

Crystal was in shock. Marcie wasn't. She leaned forward and hissed, "What if we make you another gross sandwich? Then what, Frank?"

"I'll eat it," Frank said in his show-off voice. "Any sandwich Crystal makes is fine with me."

"Oh, Romeo!" Angela cooed. She fanned herself with her hand.

Marcie leaned over and whispered something to Angela that Crystal couldn't hear. Angela started to giggle.

"What if she makes something really gross? Like peanut butter and live, juicy worms!" Angela said.

Crystal sank lower in her chair and stared at Angela. She was too miserable to say a word.

Ants were bad enough, but worms? She didn't even want to look at yucky worms, much less touch them or stir them in peanut butter or—she could hardly even think about it, it was so gruesome—spread their wiggly fat bodies on a piece of bread.

And what if she had to cut the sandwich? Double yuck! Worm guts on peanut butter.

Crystal wished her friends would keep their big mouths shut.

Too late! Frank had already taken the challenge.

"If Crystal wants to make a peanut butter and

worm sandwich," he said, loud enough so everyone in the whole third grade could hear, "I'll eat it."

Marcie stood up and put her hands on her hips. "I bet you won't!" she shouted.

"I bet I will," Frank shouted back.

Shawn and Davy pushed Frank back into his chair. Davy leaned over Frank and whispered furiously. Frank nodded and stood back up.

"It has to be Crystal," Frank said. "You girls can watch, but it has to be Crystal who actually makes the worm sandwich."

Frank closed his eyes and smiled. "And no fair cheating."

"Yeah," Shawn interrupted. "No Gummi worms or fake rubber ones. We'll check."

"No spaghetti, either," said Davy. "The worms have to be real, crawling-in-the-dirt, bloodsucking worms."

"Right," said Frank. "And they have to be mixed up with the peanut butter. They can't be just lying on the top."

Crystal thought she might be sick right on the cafeteria floor.

"And one more thing," Frank added. "I want my worm sandwich cut in half. Neatly. I don't want to have to poke dangling pieces of worm bodies and drippy chunks of peanut butter back between the bread."

Gulp! Leave it to Frank to think of everything.

Crystal turned to Marcie for help. This wasn't supposed to happen! It was Frank who was supposed to be sorry. It was Frank who was supposed to be caught in the peanut butter trap. Not her.

Chapter 7

For the rest of the afternoon Crystal tried to concentrate on her schoolwork. It was hard. She was too busy wondering how she could make a peanut butter and worm sandwich without actually touching the worms or watching them tunnel in and out of the peanut butter.

Crystal's mind wandered, but never far from worms.

Everything reminded her of worms. She saw slinky, slimy worms everywhere.

Neon-pink worms, looped in a bow, dangled from her sneakers. When Crystal shook her foot nervously, Ms. Reilly frowned. Shiny black worms were crawling through Ms. Reilly's curly hair. They were inching across her forehead!

Crystal almost fainted.

It was safer to prop her elbow on her desk, rest her chin in her hand, and stare glumly out the window. How did she ever get in this sticky peanut butter trap?

Maybe getting back at Frank wasn't such a good idea after all.

Crystal was still staring miserably out the window when Ms. Reilly called her name.

"I'm sorry to disturb you, Crystal, but if you're finished with your butterfly report, how about washing the chalkboard? I know it's not your turn, but it's two forty-five already and Ryan is still covered with papier-mâché."

Crystal put her markers away and walked to the front of the room. She took the sponge and bucket out of the closet. She turned on the faucet and filled the bucket with water.

"Do you want me to erase Frank's name?" she asked as she began sponging off the board.

Frank's name was written in bright red chalk under the big heading *DETENTION.*

Ms. Reilly glanced up from grading papers.

"Oh, no. We'll leave it there so Frank doesn't forget he has to stay after school."

Frank wouldn't forget. Crystal didn't think she'd forget either. She was the one who got Frank in trouble with Ms. Reilly.

It was her fault that Frank broke the rule about no fighting on the playground. He was only trying to protect her. He didn't want her to be embarrassed when everyone saw her bald head.

Crystal finished cleaning the chalkboard and returned to her desk. Frank was slumped in his chair, looking like a gray storm cloud.

"Walkers may go now," Ms. Reilly sang out cheerfully. "Have a nice afternoon."

The Three Musketeers stood up.

Just then Frank fell out of his desk. He rolled around on the floor and began to groan. "By the time I get home, it'll be after midnight." He hugged his stomach with both arms. "Because of certain people, I haven't eaten anything all day. Not even a crumb," he whined. "I'm starving to death and no one cares."

"That's enough, Frank," Ms. Reilly said angrily. "We all have to take responsibility for our actions. You broke a playground rule. Now you're going to be punished."

The Three Musketeers hurried out the door. Crystal thought Marcie might step on Frank first. She didn't, but only because Frank saw her coming and rolled safely off to the side.

"Okay, guys," Marcie started as soon as they got outside. "First we've got to get the worms," she said in her bossy way. "The best ones are in gardens or under logs where they can wiggle around and get juicy and fat."

Crystal felt her face turn green. It had to be green, because her stomach was upside-down.

"We can dig in my mom's garden. But we can't tell her why," Angela volunteered. "If we don't find any good worms there, we can go in the woods behind my house. That's where my brother gets his fishing worms."

"Good." Marcie sounded very organized. "Now,

what about digging things? Spoons are too small. We want really big worms for Crystal's sandwich." She paused. "Excuse me, Crystal. I mean, for *Frank's* sandwich."

Angela nodded. "My mom's got a trowel. It looks like a little shovel."

"What about a bowl?" Marcie wanted to know.

"Count me out!" Angela said. "My mom would go ballistic."

"That's okay," Marcie said. "We have tons of empty coffee cans on my dad's workbench." She turned to Crystal. "Do you still have plenty of peanut butter left?"

Crystal gulped. "Sure. Plenty."

They were more than halfway home when Davy and Shawn rode by on their bikes. Seeing them made Crystal think of Frank sitting all alone in the classroom. It made her feel awful knowing that she was responsible for getting him in trouble.

"You guys go on ahead," she said to Angela and Marcie. "I left something back in the classroom." She didn't admit that what she'd left behind was weird Frank McCormick.

Marcie frowned. "Do you want us to go with you?"

Crystal shook her head. "No. You go on and get started. I'll catch up with you at Angela's house later."

Crystal entered the red-brick school building through a side door and hurried down the empty hallway. It was so quiet. She didn't slow down until she reached the corner near the water fountain.

Someone was talking.

It sounded like Ms. Reilly.

Luckily the custodian had left a huge trash barrel outside the girls' lavatory. Crystal knelt down behind it. She peeked around the barrel.

Ms. Reilly was standing in the doorway of their classroom, talking to Frank. Crystal couldn't see Frank. She figured he was still sitting at his desk.

"No, Frank. For the hundredth time, you're not going to starve to death," Ms. Reilly said. "Your grandmother will be here shortly. You can leave as soon as you make your journal entry about why no fighting on the playground is a good rule." Ms. Reilly took a step backward. "Now continue writing. I need to check my mailbox in the front office. I'll be back in a few minutes. And Frank." Ms. Reilly paused. "Whatever you do, don't even think about moving."

Crystal waited until Ms. Reilly was safely out of sight.

Then she tiptoed around the trash barrel and into the classroom. Frank was slumped over his desk, writing in his journal.

"Pssst. Frank."

Frank put his pencil down and looked up. He was not wearing his happiest face.

"What are you doing here?" he asked.

Crystal gulped hard. She tried to think of something good to say. Nothing came to mind. "I forgot," she said instead.

"Forgot? What? Your hat?"

Crystal brightened. Leave it to Frank to come up

54

with a good excuse. "It's not my hat. It's Marcie's."

Frank picked up his pencil. He started chewing on the eraser. "That explains the cooties on Ms. Reilly's desk," he said between nibbles.

"There are no cooties." Crystal rubbed the back of her leg. "Anyway, I wanted to, uh, well, sort of say thanks."

"Thanks for what?"

"For going after that big fourth grader on the playground. The one who grabbed the hat off my head. You could have gotten really beat up."

Frank shrugged. "I didn't want you to be embarrassed, you know, with your bald head."

Crystal shrugged.

Frank chewed some more on his eraser.

Crystal waited for Frank to say something, but he didn't. Maybe she would have to go first. "I'm sorry you got into trouble."

"Yeah."

Crystal couldn't stop herself. "But none of this would have happened if you had apologized for putting bubble gum in my hair."

"Like I really meant to mess up your hair."

"Well, maybe you didn't *mean* to, but . . ."

"Look, I'm sorry," Frank said suddenly. "And I've been thinking. You don't have to make me that worm sandwich if you don't want to."

"Really?" Crystal was surprised.

"I don't even know why I said that. It was dumb."

Crystal giggled with relief. "Maybe not dumb,

exactly. But it was weird. Besides, I really hate yucky worms."

"Me too." Frank made a goofy face. "And I sure wouldn't want to have to eat any in a sandwich."

The silly way Frank said that made Crystal laugh out loud. She laughed so hard, she made a little snorting noise. That made her embarrassed. She covered her nose and mouth with both hands. She started to giggle and couldn't stop.

Frank threw back his head and laughed, a great long laugh that filled the room with sunshine.

Just then Ms. Reilly stepped back into the classroom.

"Since when is detention supposed to be funny?" she asked.

Crystal noticed the edge to Ms. Reilly's voice and gulped. She hadn't meant it to happen, but now she was in T-R-O-U-B-L-E.

Chapter

8

Crystal and Frank gave each other a worried look as Ms. Reilly clicked past them toward her desk.

"This is certainly a first," Ms. Reilly said when she turned around. "I've had students try to sneak out of detention but I've never known someone who tried to sneak in!" She smiled at Crystal. "This wouldn't have anything to do with someone's bad no-hair day, would it?"

"Sort of," Crystal said softly. "But I think my bad no-hair day is over with now."

"Well, I'm glad to hear that." Ms. Reilly motioned for Frank to bring her his journal. "Good work," she said after she'd read it.

Crystal relaxed.

"Frank," their teacher continued. "Your grandmother is waiting for you in the front office. Crystal, why don't you go along with Frank. You can use the phone to call your mother. If you haven't been home yet, she's probably concerned."

"Hey," Frank said as he slid his pencils inside his desk. "Why don't you tell your mom that you're walking home with me and my grandma? We already know where you live."

"You do?"

"Sure." Frank grinned and his dimple flashed. "I ride my bike past your house all the time."

Crystal grabbed her backpack off the floor. She didn't know what to say.

The deserted halls seemed to brighten as Crystal and Frank headed toward the office. Here and there golden streams of sunlight shone though classroom windows and splashed on the floor. Crystal felt better now that she and Frank had both said they were sorry.

Suddenly Frank's stomach growled ferociously.

"Wow!" Crystal said. "Did you make that noise all by yourself? You must be really hungry."

"Like I said, I'm starving." Frank slung his book bag over his shoulder. "I could use at least two handfuls of cookies."

"Don't look at me," Crystal said. "I don't have any. But we usually have some at my house, if you want to come over." She thought of what her mother said about talking to Frank. "Don't worry," she added. "I'll tell my mom you apologized for the bubble gum."

"What about Angela and Marcie?"

Crystal laughed. "They went on a worm hunt. Marcie really wanted you to eat worms."

Frank made a gruesome face as he wiped pretend sweat off his forehead. "Whew! That was a close call."

Crystal laughed again.

"Hey," she said after a moment. "Why don't we make our own cookies? That way we could add some really neat ingredients!"

"Like what?"

"Oh, you know. Stuff. Things that look gross and crunchy but really aren't. Then we can let everybody think we're eating bugs."

Frank pointed his finger at Crystal. "Like peanut butter and caterpillars?"

"Or peanut butter and beetles!" Crystal exclaimed.

"Or . . . peanut butter and cockroaches," they both shouted at once.

Frank put his hands up to his head and wiggled his fingers like antennas. His eyes sparkled.

Crystal laughed out loud. Frank was so funny. And cute. Now that they were friends, everything was terrific.

Tomorrow she and Frank would be stuck in the peanut butter trap—together.

Wow! Wouldn't that be fun!

Crystal and Frank's Peanut Butter Cookies

You can make your own peanut butter cookies, just like Crystal and Frank do! Here is a simple recipe for you to follow. **Make sure an adult is in the kitchen to help you.**

PEANUT BUTTER COOKIES

What you need—

1/2 cup shortening
1/2 cup brown sugar
1/2 cup granulated sugar
1 egg
1 cup creamy peanut butter
1/2 teaspoon salt
1/2 teaspoon baking soda
1/2 teaspoon vanilla
1 cup all-purpose flour

What to do—

1. Ask an adult to preheat the oven to 375° F.
2. In a bowl, mix the shortening, brown sugar, and granulated sugar until creamy.

3. Beat in the egg, peanut butter, salt, baking soda, and vanilla.

4. Sift flour and add it to the mixture to make dough.

5. Grease a cookie sheet with a little bit of shortening.

6. Roll the dough into small balls and place about one inch apart on the cookie sheet. Press the balls flat with a fork.

7. Ask an adult to put the cookies in the oven. Bake for 10 to 12 minutes.

If you want your cookies to look like they have ants in them, add chocolate sprinkles!